Toffee turns 1

CW00456942

Henry Farrell

Alpha Editions

This edition published in 2023

ISBN : 9789362095763

Design and Setting By
Alpha Editions
www.alphaedis.com
Email - info@alphaedis.com

As per information held with us this book is in Public Domain.
This book is a reproduction of an important historical work. Alpha Editions uses the
best technology to reproduce historical work in the same manner it was first
published to preserve its original nature. Any marks or number seen are left
intentionally to preserve its true form.

TOFFEE TURNS THE TRICK

BY CHARLES F. MYERS

**The fixage pills caused a major
change in Marc's life—they not only made
him a babe in arms—but Toffee's to boot!**

The strange valley, its glossy emerald carpet unruffled and unmarked, its scattered groves of odd, feathery trees undisturbed by the blue mists languishing at their feet, lay dozing in the diffused light of a sunless sky. Then, at the crest of a distant knoll, the mists suddenly stirred and gave way to a slender, gold-sandaled foot which was neatly attached to a really top-notch leg.

The leg swung gracefully into view and was instantly joined by various other notable appointments; another exquisite leg, for instance, a body of disquieting shapeliness and a pert young face. As an almost needless bonus there were also two vivid green eyes, a full red mouth and a plethora of gleaming titian hair. Together, these dazzling bits of merchandise added up to Toffee, blithe mistress of the valley of Marc Pillsworth's subconscious mind.

Certainly, Marc Pillsworth was not the first man to have a girl on his mind but at least he could claim the distinction of being the first to have one actually dwelling therein!

The girl paused a moment, gazed at the glowing sky and frowned. Barely discernible in the distance, a number of tiny storm clouds had bunched themselves together and were rapidly being joined by more of their kind. Thoughtfully Toffee started down the slope and across the valley, her slender hips weaving an indolent rhythm beneath the green transparency of her brief tunic.

She watched the gathering clouds with mixed emotions. They meant, of course, that Marc was suffering some sort of mental annoyance, some sort of anxiety ... and for that she was sorry. On the other hand, however, they might also be an indication that she was soon to be released into the world of actuality, a prospect that delighted her beyond words. Compared to the well ordered tranquility of Marc Pillsworth's subconscious, the outer world seemed to her a wonderful region of boundless pleasures and delightful excitements. If there was even a remote possibility that she was soon to be materialized in that glittering world she wanted to know about it at the earliest possible moment.

Crossing the valley, reaching the rising slopes at its outer boundaries, she turned into a sharp ravine and stopped. Ahead lay the region of Marc's conscious mind, and she could not enter there, she could only watch from the distance and wait.

Marc's conscious mind ... at least the portion of it that was visible to Toffee ... was like nothing so much as a great, dark cavern. At one end, however, the darkness was relieved by a large circular screen-like arrangement that reflected scenes and images with a penetrating, third dimensional clarity. These reflections were, of course, of the innumerable things upon which Marc gazed throughout the day. Looking at the screen from within was like looking through a great, round window.

As Toffee watched, the screen registered only a blank expanse of ceiling. Then the scene shifted abruptly, and an oak panel slid into view. A blur followed. Then a window. The window remained a moment, then skidded nervously out of range to be replaced by an eager, hawk-featured face.

Behind Toffee the storm clouds began to thicken and multiply more swiftly.

The face on the screen was furiously animated, the mouth wagging away at a terrific clip. Toffee couldn't hear the words that were the result of this frantic facial activity, but she could watch closely and try to read the lips.

In his private office in the Pillsworth Advertising Agency, Marc Pillsworth stared fixedly at the little man as though trying to will him out of existence. The fellow had been yammering at him steadily for half an hour and had yet to show the first signs of weakening. Marc's gaze wavered and moved wearily to the small green bottle standing before him on the desk. He sighed.

"Just think of it!" the little man was saying. "All humanity will be fairly trampling itself, trying to get *Fixage*. And you will be in on the ground floor for a whole twenty-five percent! Think of it!"

"I don't want to think of it," Marc muttered, then, realizing with a start that he had actually managed to get a word in edgewise, he pressed his advantage. "As I understand it, Mr. Culpepper, you want me to bring this ... uh ... this ..." he waggled a finger at the bottle on the desk "... to the attention of the manufacturers in the interests of gaining a backer. In exchange for this service you will make me a quarter owner of the invention." He fixed the little man with a severe gaze. "In other words, you haven't been able to slither through a single door with the thing ... except mine. And no wonder, if you ask me. Pills that are supposed to make a person immortal are just too...."

The little man held up an arresting hand. "You misunderstand!" he cried. "They don't make you immortal. Mercy, no! Nothing as fantastic as that. Oh, they might prolong your life twenty years or so, but their main effect is to arrest physical deterioration. In other words.... How old are you, Mr. Pillsworth?"

"Thirty-two," Marc sighed. "But it seems more like fifty."

"Thirty-two! You're right at the peak!"

"If I were at the peak," Marc said, "I would jump off."

"Just think!" the man continued. "Just think what it would mean if you could remain thirty-two for the rest of your life! Even if you live to be a hundred and thirty-two! See what I mean? No loss of faculties. No decrease in vigor. Thirty-two till the day you die! And look at the commercial value of the thing. The women. My word, the women! There isn't a woman alive who wouldn't pauperize her husband and family for a thing like Fixage. They'd be young and beautiful forever!"

"Or young and ugly," Marc murmured. With an air of finality he gripped the edge of his desk and boosted himself to his feet. "And besides, Mr. Culpepper, this agency is not interested in ventures of this sort. Frankly, I don't see why you came to me at all. When you've a proven product, fully backed and on the market, I will be happy to do business with you. But not until. It's my job to sell things to the public, not the manufacturers."

Seemingly out of nowhere, the little man's finger darted toward Marc's face. "Those wrinkles, Mr. Pillsworth!" the little man rasped. He looked as though he'd just opened the door on a closet full of vampires. "Those marks of worry and age around your eyes! They can be stopped! Permanently!"

Marc backed away, affrighted. For a moment he was very close to hiding his face in his hands. He recovered his poise just in time however.

"This is incredible," he said with hostile dignity. "My wrinkles were come by honestly, Mr. Culpepper, and if you don't mind, I'd prefer not to have them pointed at. Also, I'll thank you to stop talking in headlines and get out of my life and my office. You've already talked me out of my lunch hour and I've a great deal of work to do."

At last Mr. Culpepper seemed to get the idea. He shrugged and turned partly away.

"Oh, well," he said. "I'm willing to wait until you've made up your mind. In the meantime, I'll just leave that bottle with you, and you can think it over. You could even try it yourself and see how it works. You'll be surprised what it will do for you."

"You'll be surprised what I'll do for it," Marc said, "if you leave it here." He picked the bottle up and started around the desk with it. "Here, take it with you. I don't want you to have any excuse to come creeping back in here. Do you have your hat?"

But now the little man was as anxious to leave as Marc was to have him leave. He raced to the door and threw it open.

"Just keep it," he called back. "I'll drop back in a few days." And just before closing the door, he added, "I don't wear a hat."

Marc returned to the desk and sank into his chair. He deposited the bottle before him and regarded it thoughtfully. "Holy smoke," he murmured, "where do they come from, these crackpot ideas?"

The door opened and Memphis McGuire, Marc's secretary, bounded into the room. She was a large, healthy girl with an equally large and healthy contempt for formal office procedures. She hadn't had a decent girdle since the war.

"Hi, boss man," she said airily. "You look awful. What's the big beef?"

"I feel awful," Marc said. "Whatever possessed you to let that little creep in here? Or is this Ground Hog Day?"

"He talked so loud and so fast and so crazy," Memphis said, "I thought he might be a genius. Besides, he kept pointing at my wrinkles in front of the rest of the girls, and a lady can take just so much of that sort of thing. I had to get rid of him somehow. Get on your nerves?"

Marc nodded. "Got on 'em and stayed on 'em. My head is splitting."

"That's bad," Memphis said. "Old man Wheeler just called about his soft drink account. He's on his way over. If you're in bad shape now you'll be in ruins when he gets through with you. We'll have to get you in condition for the attack. Here, come over and stretch out on the lounge and close your eyes."

Marc did as he was told. No use arguing when Memphis was in a Nightingale mood. The secretary made retreating and returning noises and then, without warning, shocked Marc's brow with a damp cloth. She pressed a glass of water into one of his hands and two pills into the other.

"Swallow those down," she commanded. "I'll take the glass when you've finished."

Marc obeyed. "Thanks," he said.

"Glad you had some aspirin handy," Memphis said, starting to move away. "I was plum out."

"Yeah," Marc murmured. Then he sat up. "What!"

It struck him, all of a sudden, that he hadn't any aspirin either. A chill went through him. He opened his eyes and glanced at the desk, and his heart accepted an invitation to the rhumba. The little green bottle had moved to the edge of the desk and it was open!

"Memphis!"

Memphis was standing in the doorway. "Shut up," she said. "Lie down, take it easy. I'll stall Wheeler in the waiting room and feed him raw meat to dull his appetite."

She closed the door behind her.

Marc made the length of the room without once noticeably touching the floor. He grabbed the bottle and stared at its label. "*Take one,*" it instructed, "*every six months.*"

Panic crept across the silent room, but Marc forced it back.

"Oh, well," he murmured, "there's probably nothing to it. Couldn't be."

Then it hit him.

The nausea came in waves, each one growing deeper and more relentless than the last. Everything was suddenly edged in black and gold, and slowly the room began to sway. Marc felt his knees go weak and he started back toward the lounge, stumbling; if he was going to die, he might as well do it in style. He might have cried out only his throat was suddenly dry and stiff.

Toffee fled across the valley and darted into a tiny grove of trees just as the last faint glow in the sky gave way to complete darkness. A driving wind lashed the trees above her in frenetic rhythm, and the darkness was suddenly split by a writhing streak of white lightning. Her hair whipped stingingly across her face, and her tunic pressed flat against her body until it was like a part of her. Her expression, if it could have been seen, was a curious mixture of terror and exhilaration. She steadied herself against a tree and turned into the wind so that her hair blew away from her eyes. She peered into the darkness and waited.

She didn't have to wait long; the storm lasted only a moment and then it was gone. All at once the darkness was replaced by the same diffused glow that had prevailed before its coming, and the valley had returned to its former state of drowsy tranquility. Toffee emerged from the grove and surveyed the valley with expectant eyes. She was not disappointed; a lank figure lay crumpled at the bottom of the knoll. With a little cry of gladness, she ran toward it.

"Marc!" she cried. She threw herself down beside him on the grass. "You divine devil, you! I've been expecting you all day." In a burst of enthusiasm, she threw her arms around him and hugged him to her.

Marc opened his eyes and frowned. "Handle with care," he said thickly. "I think I'm fragile." He glanced around at the valley and his face registered recognition. "So I'm back here again, am I? I'm not dead then."

"You drew a blank," Toffee said. "It was a daisy, too. This valley wasn't fit for man nor any other kind of beast when you hit it. What happened?"

Marc boosted himself forward and ran a lean hand through his sandy hair. "I don't remember," he said. "It must have been terrific, I feel all twisted up inside."

"Just a little shaken up," Toffee said confidently. "You'll be all right. Tell me, just to make conversation, how's your wife? That big blonde?"

"Away," Marc said. "Julie went to Kansas to look after an ailing relative. A cousin, I believe."

Toffee nodded with satisfaction. "Good," she said. "That leaves me a free field, doesn't it?" The speculation in her eyes was undisguised. "We will have fun. Lots."

"Now look here," Marc said, trying to look firm. "Let's not have any horsing around. Just this once why don't you stay here, where you belong? Just because I dream you up that doesn't mean that you have to come popping into my life, messing it up. Be reasonable."

"Sure," Toffee said. "I'll be reasonable ... dirt cheap, if need be. I'll listen to any proposition you may have to make ... if it's not too respectable." She twined her arms around his neck. "Kiss me. All this dull talk is beginning to tire me."

Marc was in the midst of shoving her away from him when the storm returned. It came as suddenly and as mysteriously as it had departed, lashing the trees on the knoll against each other, driving the light from the sky. In a sudden start of surprise, Marc clutched Toffee to him.

"Why, you impetuous old rogue!" Toffee cried. "What a clutch!"

For a moment they clung together, helpless under the driving blast of the wind. Then they felt themselves being lifted, as by a giant hand, and hurled into space.

A vari-colored pin-wheel whirled through the darkness and struck Marc squarely between the eyes. Instantly his mind cleared a little, and he opened his eyes. A strip of oak paneling met his gaze, its dark grains writhing before him like water snakes in a pond. He turned over on the lounge and looked at the room. Slowly the room and its objects fell into place and became fixed. He flinched.

Toffee smiled down at him. "Greetings," she said. "Always flat on your back, aren't you?"

Marc gazed at the girl and her brief tunic without pleasure; it was a sight that shocked his finer sensibilities. Surrounded by the severity of the office she looked even more naked somehow than she really was. Absently he tried to imagine her in a more suitable background, but the only setting that occurred to him was one that featured a great deal of plumbing and running water. His mind veered away from a vision that thoroughly repelled him.

"Go 'way," he said. "If you have any shame at all, go 'way and hide yourself. I don't want to look at you."

"You should be so lucky," Toffee retorted. "And don't try pulling any of your phony moralistic airs on me. Remember, I know what's in your mind." She sat down on the edge of the lounge. "How do you feel?"

Marc sat up and considered. He examined his emotions and state of health with care, and was soundly surprised at his findings.

"I feel wonderful!" he exclaimed. "I feel great!"

"Who boffed you?" Toffee asked.

"Boffed?" Marc asked. "How do you mean?" He thought back, trying to remember. "Oh, that!" he said finally. His gaze wandered to the green bottle on the desk. "Those pills. I took a couple." He laughed shortly. "They hit me like a sledge hammer, but they don't seem to have had any serious effects. Memphis gave them to me by mistake just before...." His eyes widened. "Oh, my gosh! How long have I been out? Old man Wheeler may walk in here any moment! He mustn't see you!"

"Who's Wheeler?" Toffee asked.

"A client. He's about sixty-eight and as...."

"I'll leave," Toffee said. "When they get past sixty I begin to lose interest ... and patience."

Marc took her by the arm and started her across the room. "You can take the rear door," he said. "It leads to the hallway and.... Stop twitching your hips like that. When you get outside...."

He stopped and made a small whining noise.

It was as though the ceiling had suddenly come crashing down around his head. For a moment he was numb all over. Then he could feel himself sinking toward the floor, but he wasn't falling. The sensation was alarmingly strange and disagreeable.

"What the devil's...!"

He stopped again; his voice was echoing back to him in an unfamiliar falsetto. The words were his but the voice definitely was not. He started back in alarm, tripped over something and sat down heavily on the floor. It was then that he glanced up and saw Toffee. For a moment he was certain he was losing his mind.

Instead of the well-curved, half-clad redhead he had last seen, he was now confronted by a chunky little moppet of about eight. Her heretofore inadequate tunic now covered her completely, part of it even trailing on the floor. He opened his mouth to speak but gave it up as Toffee expressed his emotions for him with a shrill scream of dismay. Apparently unmindful of her sudden transformation, however, she was staring at him with horror.

"You've shrunk!" she cried. "You've ... you've shriveled!"

Her voice, also, had moved up an octave or so.

Marc quickly turned his attention to his own person and found to his complete stupefaction that Toffee spoke the truth. Indeed he had shrunk like a ten-dollar suit in a cloudburst. What he had tripped over had been his own trouser legs, the spare yardage of which was wadded loosely about his ankles.

"Those pills!" he yelped. "Good grief! They've not only stopped my age, they've backed it up!"

Toffee giggled a little hysterically. "You look so funny!" she tittered. "Your ears are so big. And ... and you've got freckles!"

Marc winced; it was probably all too true. As a youngster he had been plagued with these disfigurements and he had been very sensitive about them. After all, being called "pitcher ears" and "leopard puss" hadn't been fun. Outgrowing these names had been his own personal triumph. And now all that was cancelled; he was back where he had started. He looked up woundedly.

"Look who's laughing," he said. "With that pot belly of yours, you're no glamour item yourself."

An expression of utmost horror swept Toffee's face as she ceased to stare at Marc and turned her attention to herself. One quick, shuddering glance told her the story. This time she screamed as though she really meant it.

"No!" she shrieked. "No! NOooooh! It isn't *me*! It *isn't*!" She turned on Marc, raging. "You did this! You swallowed those crazy pills!" Irrationally, she held her hand under his mouth. "Spit them out!" she demanded. "Spit them out this instant or I'll rip those revolting ears right off your despicable head!"

"Don't be disgusting," Marc said, looking away.

"You'll be surprised how disgusting I can really be," Toffee wailed, "if you don't do something about this."

"What can I do?" Marc asked helplessly. "After all the pills were Culpepper's idea, not mine. He's the only one that can do anything about it."

"Get him!" Toffee cried. "Get him! Ring him, call him, wire him, cable him! Only get him!" Her cherubic face began to pucker, her large eyes beginning to cloud. "Wouldn't you know that I'd have to suffer too, just because you were simple-minded enough to take a couple of pills! Wouldn't you know? Look at me! ... just a shapeless little chunk of blubber. I've got about as much appeal as a smudge pot. Less!"

"Stop your sniveling," Marc said crossly. "It isn't helping matters. And I've got to think."

"Why start now?" Toffee asked waspishly.

Marc thoughtfully rolled up his trousers and got to his feet. Full length, he was even stranger to look upon than when sitting down.

His coat sleeves hung limp at his sides, extending nearly a foot beyond his hands; his shirt collar, previously a perfect fit, was now a perfect scream; his scrawny neck jutted out of it like a wire coat hanger. When he walked, his shoes shifted loosely about his feet, making an annoying clattering noise against the floor. Marc Pillsworth, taken all in all, which really wasn't so very much as things stood, had suddenly become an offense to both eye and ear. Toffee, who, on the other hand, had retained a goodly portion of her comeliness, regarded him with distaste.

"If we ever get out of this, pitcher ears," she said, "I hope you have to go through your adolescence again."

Suddenly they both jumped as the door opened and Memphis' head jutted into the room. The secretary opened her mouth to say something, then froze, goggle-eyed. She stared blankly at Marc and Toffee, and they, for want of anything better, simply stared back. There was a long moment of super-charged silence before Memphis found her voice.

"Wh ... ," she said weakly. "Where's Mr. Pillsworth?"

Toffee laughed bitterly. "That jerk," she murmured.

Memphis smiled stiffly. "I don't know how you got in here, honey," she said with false sweetness, "but you really shouldn't be here; this is a business office."

"You're telling me?" Toffee said. "I'm the kid that got the business in it."

Memphis cleared her throat. "Now why don't you just tell me where Mr. Pillsworth has gone and then run along and play?"

Toffee turned to Marc. "Listen to that overstuffed tomato giving us the rush act," she said. She cast glittering eyes toward Memphis. "For two cents I'd come over there and hammer your big thick shins for you. And if you don't clear out I may decide to do it for free. Beat it yourself. You're bothering us."

Memphis gasped. Then she turned to Marc. "Tell me, sonny," she said, "how does your sister like her spankings ... sunny side up or over easy? Or are you a wiseacre too? Now, look here...." She stopped short as her gaze fell on Marc's sagging costume. Her eyes grew wise and fearful. "You're wearing Mr. Pillsworth's suit!" she shrieked. "What have you done to him?"

"You'd be surprised, Bertha," Toffee sneered. "In my opinion it wasn't half what he deserved."

For a moment Memphis was struck dumb. Then her voice came back to her in a lusty scream. She wheeled around and charged out of the room. A second later there was the sound of a telephone dial being put into frenzied motion. Memphis was bawling for the police even as she dialed.

Marc, who had remained in a state of mental and physical paralysis during this disquieting interview, suddenly came to life.

"Now see what you've done!" he piped in his child's voice. "Why couldn't you tell her the truth?"

"She'd have to be daffy to believe it," Toffee said. "Besides, I didn't like her attitude; she was treating me like a child."

"Now we'll have to run for it," Marc said. "Once the police get hold of us, we'll never find Culpepper."

They left the office through the rear door and made their way quickly down the hall to the fire escape window. Marc pointed to a blue convertible in the parking lot below.

"We'll have to try to drive the thing somehow," he said. "After we've gotten away, we'll do what we can about getting in touch with Culpepper."

"I'd like to get in touch with him," Toffee lisped, "with a crowbar."

As Marc was boosting Toffee over the sill and onto the fire escape, a nearby door opened and a large, florid woman stepped into the hallway. She stopped at the sight of the children and observed their activities with alarm.

"Here, here, kiddies," she said, looking maternal, "you mustn't play out there; you might get hurt. Where are your mummy and daddy?"

"Down at the hoosegow," Toffee said evilly. "Mummy's bailing daddy out for peddling hashish at the orphans' picnic. What's it to you?"

"Oh, dear!" the woman exclaimed. "You poor, little, neglected, underprivileged things!" She started forward but was suddenly stopped by a warning glance from Toffee.

"Better stay out of this, fatso," Toffee cooed. "You might get your girdle fractured."

The woman turned red. Then she swung around and continued abruptly down the hall. "Little monsters!" she snorted. "Hope they break their dirty, little underprivileged necks!"

Away from the building and in the car, the two inadvertent juveniles found themselves at sharp odds with the mechanical age. Squatting on the floor, Toffee attempted to operate the foot mechanisms while Marc knelt on the seat and tried his small hand at manipulating the steering apparatus and gear shift. After much concentrated effort and grinding of gears they managed jointly to smash the fender of the neighboring sedan. There the operation ended in dismal failure. Time was running out like water in a hair net. Memphis, in the company of two uniformed companions, was gesticulating wildly from a fourth story window.

"Delinquents!" she yelled. "Juvenile fiends! Now they're stealing his car!"

"Duck down!" Toffee rasped. She reached up and pulled Marc down beside her. "Stay out of sight!"

"They've already spotted us," Marc returned. "They'll be down here in a moment." He reached past her and opened the car door. "Crawl out," he instructed. "I'll follow. We can crawl along under the cars."

Like a couple of bemused slugs, they scooted out of the car, under the sedan of the abused bumper and started on a scenic tour of gravel and axles. They had removed themselves from the convertible by only five cars when the sound of flat feet scraping over gravel sullied the quiet afternoon air. Toffee, leading the way, peered fearfully from beneath the fender of their current refuge.

"They're closing in," she said. "They've searched your car and now they're fanning out. What'll we do?"

Marc thrust his wide-eared countenance next to Toffee's and surveyed the situation. The policemen, under the supervision of Memphis, were embarked upon a campaign to beat every inch of automotive brush in the entire parking lot. Currently, however, these activities had been arrested by the arrival of the parking lot attendant who, quite understandably, was wanting to know just what was going on. Still the situation looked grim for Marc and Toffee once the search was resumed ... as it would be in only a second ... the jig was up. Marc glanced quickly around for possible avenues of escape.

The vehicle next to the one under which they were hiding was a large delivery truck with paneled sides. It was black and rather formidable looking but still it offered a possibility.

"Over there," Marc whispered, pointing to the truck. "Crawl under and toward the back. We can open the rear doors and climb inside without being seen."

Toffee nodded and started out. When they arrived at the rear of the truck, they managed to open the doors and get inside with a certain amount of cooperative pushing and pulling. They closed the doors after them and Marc found an inside catch with which the doors could be locked. They settled back in the dimness to catch their breath.

A removable panel isolated the rear compartment from the driver's cab, cutting off most of the light, and the two fugitives had to feel their way about.

"There's a bundle of rags or something over here," Toffee whispered presently. "Anyway, it's soft. Come on over and sit down."

Marc groped his way across the truck, found the bundle and sat down at Toffee's side.

"Guess there's nothing to do now," he said, "but wait for the worst."

"In the meantime," Toffee said, "what are we going to do about this kiddie business? I don't like it."

"You don't like it," Marc sighed. "I don't like it. And come to think of it, I don't suppose my wife will go for it much either."

"Ouch!" Toffee cried suddenly. "Stop it! This is no time for that sort of thing."

"What sort of thing?"

"You pinched me, you big ... little oaf, and you know it."

"I haven't layed a hand on you," Marc said. "In your present condition, why should I? You flatter yourself."

"Oh yeah?" Toffee said. "I've heard about nasty little boys who run around pinching little girls. If you do it again...."

From outside there was the sound of approaching footsteps. They moved to the rear of the truck and suddenly the door handles began to rattle. Then they stopped, and a voice called out, "Not in here. All locked up." The footsteps moved away, into the distance.

"Anyway," Toffee said, getting back to the matter of the pinchings, "you keep your offensive little paws to yourself from now on or I'll snap them off."

"You back on that?" Marc asked wearily. "Even in childhood you're dirty-minded, aren't you? One would think that.... Ow! Of all the spiteful things to do!"

"What did I do?"

"As if you didn't know, tubby," Marc said nastily. "Pinching me behind my back. Literally!"

"I didn't," Toffee said. "Behind your back or anywhere else. I was too busy massaging my own...."

"Hissst!"

"Now what?" Marc asked.

"Hissst!"

"Stop that silly hisssting, will you?" Toffee said irritably. "You sound crazy. Probably look it, too."

"Who's hissting?" Marc asked. "I haven't made a sound."

"Hissst!"

Both of them were suddenly on their feet.

"Oh, mother!" Toffee moaned. "Snakes! We're in a pit of snakes. Just listen to the beasts. They're fairly lusting for us!"

"Moses!" Marc gasped. "We've been bitten and hissed at by snakes!"

They froze as the dark compartment suddenly came alive with heavy thumping sounds, intermingled with, "Hisst! Hisssst! Hissssst!"

"Pythons!" Toffee whinnied. And all but falling over herself, she lunged to the door and threw the catch.

"The cops!" Marc cried. "What about the cops? They're still out there."

"Right now," Toffee said positively, "there is nothing I would love better than a big, tough cop. I'm going to fling myself on the very first one I see and never let go. I'm going to love that ugly cop like a mother."

She threw the door open, and the compartment flooded with light. She was just about to jump to the ground when she glanced quickly back over her shoulder and stopped.

"Look!" she cried, pointing back into the compartment. "It's human!"

For a moment they simply stared at the transformed bundle of rags. In the light it had suddenly developed a head, arms and legs. It was lying on its stomach with its face turned painfully toward them. A crude gag covered the lower half of its face and its hands were lashed behind its back, which probably explained the mysterious pinchings. The feet were bound together like the hands. It said, "Hisst!"

Marc and Toffee ran to it. They knelt beside it, and Marc untied the gag. A small hawk-like face peered up at them.

"Culpepper!" Marc gasped. He turned to Toffee. "It's a snake after all."

The little man sighed with relief. "Hurry and untie me," he said. "They'll kill me."

"And I'll help them," Marc said.

The little man blinked. "How's that?" he asked.

"I'm Pillsworth," Marc said. "Look at me."

"Ah, yes," the little man said. "Mr. Pillsworth's son. I see the resemblance, though your mother must have been an exceptionally large-eared woman. Untie me, sonny, and...."

Marc choked. "Don't sonny me, you degenerate genius," he grated. "I'm Marc Pillsworth, the Marc Pillsworth you were chattering to death in his office a little while ago, the Marc Pillsworth who used to be over six feet tall, so that his ears didn't look so big ... that's the Marc Pillsworth I am, butter brain. I took a couple of your pills. Look at me, you monster!"

"What!" The little man struggled to sit up under his bonds. "You *what*!"

"Took a couple of your pills. And frankly, Mr. Culpepper, I am not satisfied with the results. I want my money ba.... I mean, you've got to get us out of this. My wife isn't going to understand."

"Us?" the little man asked. He glanced at Toffee. "Her, too?"

Marc nodded. "You'd better whip out an antidote or I'll turn you over to whoever is trying to kill you before you can say corpus delicti. I'll even loan them my old blunderbuss which is guaranteed to blast a hole a foot deep in a wall of solid concrete."

"An antidote?" the little man said. "I don't have one. I've been working on one, but I haven't thought it out completely yet. If you'll just get me out of here, I promise to do what I can."

"Untie him," Toffee said, already grappling with the ropes round his ankles. "Hurry."

Marc nodded and set to work on Mr. Culpepper's wrists. "Who's trying to kill you?" he asked.

"Mr. and Mrs. Harper," the little man said. "They want my formula for Fixage. I met them down in the Marlborough district. It's a pretty bad neighborhood. My laboratory is down there in an old building, I couldn't afford anything better. Anyway, I met these people one night ... I guess I was drinking a little too much ... and I told them about Fixage and how I was going to make a fortune with it. They were quite impressed. Ah, my dear, that feels good. My feet had nearly gone to sleep."

"Go on," Marc said. "What about the Harpers?"

"Well, I could tell they'd had plastic surgery done on their faces, and I guess I should have suspected them right away. Illegal treatment, you know, thrives down in that part of town. I think maybe they've escaped from the penitentiary or something, but there's no way of identifying them. They broke into my laboratory several times, but I didn't know who it was until now. They're planning to steal my formula and kill me and say they invented Fixage themselves. They followed me here today somehow and grabbed me when I came out."

"Where are they now?"

"They saw me carrying a brief case into the building and they think I've hidden it in there. They've gone back to look for it."

"Where is it?" Marc asked.

The little man chuckled. "In the men's room," he said. "I forgot and left it. They'll never find it there."

"Good night!" Marc said. "Someone else might. Is the formula in it?"

"Oh, no," the little man said. "There's nothing in it but my dirty laundry. I never put my experiments on paper."

"Where is the formula?"

Mr. Culpepper smiled. "In my head," he said. "I work everything out in my head. I just go into a kind of trance and things start coming to me. I don't really need a laboratory at all but it makes a better impression to have one. I just go down there and cook up a pot of coffee once in a while for the sake of appearances."

At last Marc unraveled the snarl of knots about the little man's wrists. "There you are," he said. "Let's go."

He proceeded to the door of the truck and peeked out. Memphis and the policeman were at a safe distance and seemed too involved in a heated argument to notice anything else. Marc lowered himself to the ground and turned back, holding out his arms. "Here, I'll help you down," he said to Toffee. "Just give me your...."

"Now isn't that obliging?" a man's voice said smoothly behind him. "The little tyke's put his hands up without even being told. Good training will tell every time, Agatha, I've always said it."

Something cold and round nuzzled Marc's spine with unrequited affection.

"He shows splendid manners," a woman's voice returned, "for one so young."

Just then Toffee appeared in the doorway. "Oh, my gosh!" she said.

Behind Marc, both holding pistols in gloved hands, were a man and woman of truly stunning elegance. The man was tall and straight and beautifully tailored ... a gentleman down to the last hand-woven thread. The woman at his side was dark and svelte, and her soft grey suit was so Parisian that her figure was plainly speaking French beneath it. Both of these prepossessing creatures were graced with extraordinary handsome faces. Faint scars whispered the truth; something other than nature had worked these perfections.

"Mr. and Mrs. Harper, I presume?" Toffee drawled, eyeing the guns. "I'm sorry I didn't expect to meet you folks or I'd have fixed up a bit. I must look a mess without my diamond tiara and tommy gun."

The woman eyed Toffee with disdain. "What an offensive child," she murmured. Her words were clipped and exaggeratedly European. "Really, Chadwick, if she keeps on like this, I'm afraid I'll be tempted to do her in."

Chadwick regarded Marc and Toffee with dulled eyes. "It's a sad thing," he said morosely, "when we have to deal with such low types."

"Ah, yes," Agatha replied. "It's a situation that needs mending when we are forced to waste our talents on mere moppets. However ..." she shrugged philosophically "... things will be better when we've gotten the old man's formula. I wonder how they came here?"

"Search me, love."

"Don't ever say that," Agatha warned, "Someone might take you up on it."

"S'pose you're right," Chadwick mused. He jostled his gun in Marc's back. "There's a good lad," he said. "Let's hop back in there."

Marc hopped and found himself once more in the more comforting company of Toffee and Mr. Culpepper.

"The Harpers," Mr. Culpepper explained wryly, "are charming people."

"Yes," Toffee said. "Charming, like an emerald-studded hand grenade."

"Culpepper's come untied," Chadwick said outside. "I suppose you'd better ride with them and keep them covered whilst I drive."

"What a bother," the woman lamented. "Oh, well, hand me up."

Chadwick lifted Agatha to the compartment and she stepped lightly inside. Then he closed them in and took his place behind the wheel. The removable panel at the front of the truck slid down and he turned toward them.

"What will we ever do with them, Aggie?" he asked.

"The children?" Agatha said. "Oh, I don't know, dear. Dispose of them in the usual manner, I suppose."

"Yes, I suppose so," Chadwick said. "Only it really doesn't seem quite proper, you know, their being children and all, I mean."

"But they're not very pretty children," Agatha replied. "And after all, when you come right down to it, what are children except just ungrown people?"

"You may be right," Chadwick mused. "Perhaps if we use small bullets...."

"I really think we should be getting on, don't you?" Agatha broke in. "I observed several police persons at the end of the lot when we came out."

"Right-ho," Chadwick said.

"Police persons!" Toffee snorted. "Just listen! You'd think this was a garden party!"

Agatha turned to her with a slow smile. "Quite right," she said. "Tea and bullets will be served directly. And remember, should we be stopped for any reason along the way, you and your little friend will act as our children. You'll call Chadwick daddy and me mummy." She pointed to Toffee. "You're Gwendolyn and the boy is Horace. Mr. Culpepper is your uncle Ben. Understand?"

"Oh, yes," Toffee said brightly. "We're just one big stuffy family. Only if mummy drops her gun, Gwendolyn is going to kick the stuffing out of her, and don't you forget it, sister."

Agatha shuddered delicately. "Please," she said. "Unless you watch your language a bit more closely I'm afraid I'll have to wash your mouth out with cyanide."

Toffee retired to a corner and sat down, folding her arms dispiritedly over her chest. "I wash my hands of this whole affair," she mumbled. "This is the most boring stick-up I've ever been in."

The occasion, thankfully, did not arise for Marc and Toffee to use their unlikely aliases. Uninterrupted, save by traffic lights, the black delivery truck made its way from the center of the city into an old commercial district of derelict buildings and littered streets. Chadwick turned the truck in at an alleyway and pulled to a stop behind an aging, disreputable-looking warehouse. He got out of the car long enough to open a pair of huge barn-like doors and returned to drive the vehicle inside. The little party alighted, and the newcomers were given a brief moment to inspect their surroundings before the doors were closed again, shutting out most of the light.

Bare rafters lay high above them and all the windows had been boarded over. Along the right hand wall a rickety stairway stretched upward to a kind of landing, the outer edge of which was lined with a mouldering railing. Beyond the railing a blank, unpainted wall offered several doors, probably entrances to subsidiary storerooms or offices. Whatever things of value the place had once protected it now harbored only dust and disuse.

"What a lovely little nest," Toffee murmured. "It looks so died in." She turned to Agatha. "With all this, you must feel just like a bird in a gilded cage. A vulture."

"We do not live here," Agatha returned distantly. "We felt, however, that it was more than sufficient for Mr. Culpepper until we were done with him. It will do for you and your little friend, too, now that you're here." She gestured toward the stairway with her gun. "Shall we go up?"

Marc and Toffee, with Mr. Culpepper between them, started up the stairs, and Agatha, Chadwick and their pistols followed. Under their tread the ancient boards screamed threateningly, and the sound echoed weirdly all around them.

"You know, Agatha," Chadwick said suddenly, "just seeing these youngsters has made me rather thoughtful."

"Indeed?" Agatha rejoined.

"Yes, quite." A mellow tone had come into Chadwick's voice. "I was wondering, dear, if it wouldn't be rather nice if we had some children of our own. What do you think, eh?"

"I see no reason why we couldn't," Agatha said agreeably. "There are any number of really well-bred children roving the streets these days. There would be nothing to kidnapping a couple of the nicest."

"No, no," Chadwick said. "That's not what I mean. I thought we might have some that were really our own."

"How *common!*" Agatha exclaimed, truly shocked. "Really, Chadwick!"

"You've no sentiment, Aggie," Chadwick said, a shade of reproach in his voice.

"Oh, really?" Agatha said. "I suppose you've forgotten when we were getting Freddie Freemont's body ready to chuck in the channel? Wasn't it I who wrote 'Bon Voyage, Frederick' in the cement before it dried? And very pretty it was, too, what with the writing wreathing his neck as it did."

"That's right," Chadwick said. "That was quite sweet of you, Aggie."

"I should think so," Agatha said self-righteously. "I could just as easily have written 'Fry in Hell' as Bugsy Turner wanted me to. I was too sentimental, though."

At the top of the stairs Agatha, the gushing sentimentalist, directed Marc, Toffee and Mr. Culpepper into the first room to their left, with a curt wave of her gun. Apparently the room had seen service as an office at one time, for there was a sort of teller's window cut into the inner wall. There was a larger window in the opposite wall, but since it was boarded up like all the others, it offered only a bare minimum of air and light. In the center of the room an old packing crate had been turned face down so as to provide a resting place for a silver tea service and several extremely potent looking bottles. A number of fruit boxes had been distributed around the room to serve as chairs, and the floor was generously littered with mashed out cigarettes.

When her guests were seated, Agatha stood back, studied them and frowned. "Oh, Chad," she said. "They're so ordinary!"

"There, there, Aggie," Chadwick said, stroking her cheek affectionately with the nose of his gun. "In business you can't always associate with the best. It's all part of the game, you know."

"Some game," Toffee said sourly. "I could stage a better crime wave with a water pistol."

Agatha swung on Toffee, eyes blazing. "You soiled little hoyden!" she fumed. "You should be honored. Chadwick and I were the most celebrated thieves in Europe before the war. We robbed kings, I'll have you know. Our names were on aristocratic lips all through the continent."

"What's the matter?" Toffee said. "Did those aristocratic lips spit you out finally? Why didn't you stay on the continent?"

"Don't think we couldn't have," Agatha said with a little lift of her chin. "People were practically begging us to stay and rob them." She sighed. "However, they were only putting up a front; they had nothing really worth robbing. They only wanted the social prestige that one of our robberies could give them. We were forced to come to America." She made a wry face. "They're all like you here; want a lot of shooting and uncouth language with their hold-ups. No appreciation for continental finesse. That's why we've decided to take Mr. Culpepper's formula. We're going into business. It's a shameful come-down, of course, but I suppose we'll just have to make the best of it."

"You poor, brave things," Toffee said. "My nose fairly runs for you."

"Oh!" Agatha exploded. "Little pig!"

"Big pig!" Toffee shot back.

"Here, here," Chadwick broke in. "This bickering has got to stop. Really. There's business to be taken care of."

Agatha nodded and turned her attention to Mr. Culpepper. "Shall we torture it out of him?" she asked.

"I think so," Chadwick said. "That's why I've brought the pliers ... to pull his fingernails, you know. I thought it might cheer you up, old girl. Remember when we used that method on the Marquis?"

Forgetting her gun, Agatha clasped her hands together. "Oh, what a triumph!" she exclaimed. "The Marquis was simply enthralled. He said it was the most exquisite torture he'd ever experienced."

"Is everybody nuts in Europe?" Toffee asked. "Or just your particular crowd?"

No one answered her.

"What a shame," Chadwick said, "to waste such divine methods on a commoner." He removed a pair of silver, leather-encased pliers from his jacket pocket and held them out proudly. He turned to Mr. Culpepper. A look of injury spread over his handsome features.

The little scientist, far from shivering with delighted horror over his impending torture, had closed his eyes and was leaning back against the wall in an attitude of deep meditation. At his side, Marc was staring eagerly at the thoughtful face. The two seemed completely oblivious to all else except themselves.

A flame of anger flickered in Chadwick's eyes. "Oh, really!" he exclaimed. "If that's the way it's going to be, I've half a mind not to pull his nails at all. He doesn't deserve it."

Agatha moved quickly to his side. "Now, don't lose your temper, love," she said. "You must force yourself. So much depends on it."

"Oh, very well," Chadwick said sullenly. He strode to Mr. Culpepper's side and stamped his foot. "Peasant!" he sneered.

Marc looked up, startled, and quickly put a finger to his lips. "Shhh!" he said. "Culpepper's working on an antidote. If you disturb him he may not get it finished. He works everything out in his head, you know."

"Well!" Chadwick exploded. "Of all the...!" He reached down and shook the scientist's shoulder. "Wake up!" he commanded.

Mr. Culpepper opened his eyes and gazed up at Chadwick, but it was apparent that he didn't really see him. His eyes were glazed and introspective. His mouth fell open to complete an expression of sheerest idiocy.

"My word!" Agatha breathed. "What's happened to him?"

"I don't know," Chadwick said decisively, "but I do know what's *going* to happen to him." He grasped Mr. Culpepper's hand and separated the little finger from the others. "Let's see him work this out in his mind."

Now that he was getting down to business, Chadwick seemed to experience a lift in spirit. "I think this will snap him out of it." He said it like a doctor about to administer the shock treatment to a mental patient. He hummed softly to himself.

"Oh, Mona!" Toffee moaned. "Just look at him! Happy as a hophead with a new poppy patch!"

She glanced at Mr. Culpepper but the little man had closed his eyes again, completely unaware that fate had singled him out for the main attraction at a sadistic fun fest. At his side, his eyes riveted on the advancing pliers, Marc was rigid in a state of white-faced paralysis.

Toffee darted from her place just as the pliers closed over Mr. Culpepper's nail. "Stop that!" she cried. She ran to Mr. Culpepper and shook him. "Wake up!" she pleaded. "Tell them the silly formula and let them have it!"

Mr. Culpepper's mouth snapped shut, but other than that, there was no reaction. She shook him again, but with no further result. Her eyes darted to his outstretched hand, and she gasped. Chadwick was beginning to pull.

Toffee sucked in a deep breath. "I ... I'll tell!" she faltered. "I know the formula. I'll give it to you."

The pliers came apart and Mr. Culpepper's small, veined hand fell limply to the little man's side. Toffee found herself instantly and confusingly confronted by Chadwick and Agatha.

"You know the formula?" Agatha said. "You'd best not be lying."

"Why ... I...." Toffee stammered.

"Speak up!" Chadwick snapped.

"I know all about it," Toffee said. The words came in a rush. "I was his human subject. He experimented on me in his laboratory. You'd never guess that I'm really twenty years old, would you?"

The two looked at her suspiciously.

"She's lying," Agatha said. "She couldn't be twenty."

"Oh, yes," Toffee insisted, warming up to the lie. "Mr. Culpepper lured me into his laboratory with a stick of candy when I was only eight years old. I haven't aged a day since."

"Might be right at that," Chadwick mused. "After all, you'll have to admit that her language is rather advanced for just a child ... in an appalling sort of way."

"Can you prove what you say?" Agatha asked.

Toffee hesitated. "Well," she said presently, "in a way, I can. There's another thing about Fixage that you don't know."

"Yes?" Chadwick and Agatha chorused. "What's that?"

Toffee beckoned them closer and whispered, "It causes you to be immortal."

"Oh, no," Agatha said. "That's going too far."

"I'll prove it," Toffee said. "I don't suppose you'd be willing to loan me a gun for a moment?"

"Certainly not," Chadwick said. "These pistols came from the home of a duke. The fellow would never forgive us if we loaned them."

"That's what I thought," Toffee said. She shrugged. "In that case...." She started toward the door.

Marc, having come to life again when Mr. Culpepper's finger was delivered from the hand of Chadwick, suddenly ran to Toffee's side. Together they moved through the doorway, and Chadwick and Agatha followed. Mr. Culpepper, for his part, continued to slumber contentedly in his corner.

Outside on the landing, Toffee went with business-like directness to the outer railing and started to climb over it.

"Good heavens, child," Agatha said. "What are you doing?"

"I'm going to jump," Toffee said. "You'll agree, won't you, that such a fall would kill most people?"

"Oh, but you mustn't!" Agatha cried, shocked. "You'll make a mess on the floor!"

"You'll see," Toffee said. She wriggled her plump little body to the top of the railing and peered into the well of darkness beneath her.

"Stop her!" Agatha cried. "Fetch her back, Chad! She may splatter the auto and ruin the finish!"

Chadwick reached out toward Toffee, but just as his hand went to her, there was a terrible splintering sound, and the railing began to crumble. Then the railing gave way entirely and Toffee's small figure pitched forward, plunged into the darkness below.

On the landing the three tensed, then started a bit as a dull thump echoed up to them from below.

"Oh, gracious!" Agatha wailed. "I just know she struck the auto!"

"What do you suppose ever made her do it?" Chadwick mused. He shrugged. "Just suicidal, I guess, by nature."

"You'll wash the car," Agatha said adamantly. "I won't do it."

Beside them, Marc had turned away from the railing and was peering anxiously down the darkened stairway. A smile suddenly lighted his face as the ancient boards sent up their accustomed cry.

"Heavens!" Agatha said. "Whatever could it be?"

"I haven't the faintest ..." Chadwick said. "One thing, it surely couldn't be the child."

But it was the child. Emerging from the darkness, Toffee raced up the stairs, smiling and completely unmarked. For a brief instant her eyes flicked in Marc's direction and her lips silently formed the word "thanks."

Marc understood. It was only through his concentration that she had survived. As long as he was aware of her and "wished" her into being, she was indestructible. Her life could be threatened only when his was.

"Lord," Chadwick breathed. "The little waif's all right!"

"Chad!" Agatha cried, turning to him. "Do you realize what this means? We ... we ... I almost can't say it, it's so wonderful ... we can be *immortal!* All we have to do is get the formula. No one will be able to kill us! We can go where we choose, take what we like, and no one can ever stop us. Perhaps we could organize a whole band of immortals and...."

"Certainly!" Chadwick cried, catching her enthusiasm. "We could rule the world if we chose! Who would there be to stop us? We'd be indestructible!"

They turned to Toffee in unison.

"What's the formula?" Chadwick asked, beginning to look a little feverish. "Tell us what it is."

For a moment Toffee was pensive, then a touch of craftiness came into her childish face. "I'll do better than that," she said. "I'll take you to a whole bottle of the pills, all made up and ready to take."

"Wonderful!" Agatha cried.

Mr. Culpepper was suddenly recalled to them by a sudden, triumphant cry that issued from the inner reaches of the abandoned office. In a body they turned back and crowded through the door.

"Fancy that!" the little man was shouting. "Just fancy that!" A smile of amazement was on his sharp-featured face.

"Have you got it?" Marc asked, running to his side.

"I certainly have," Mr. Culpepper said happily. "It was a very difficult experiment, but I got it. And will you be surprised!"

"What has he got?" Chadwick asked.

"Perhaps it would be better not to ask," Agatha said. "From the way he's been behaving it might be anything."

Chadwick nodded. "I wouldn't be surprised. Besides, we've other fish to fry now. Let's be on our way." He started to the door. "I'll get the car started and you bring them down."

When he had gone, Agatha stepped over to the doorway and motioned with her gun. "Come, come," she said brightly. "Time to be leaving, everyone."

Toffee promptly took to the stairs, but Marc and Mr. Culpepper seemed to hesitate, too absorbed in a whispered conversation to take much note of anything else.

"You could have knocked me over with a noodle," Mr. Culpepper was saying. "I simply couldn't believe it at first."

"Well, what is it?" Marc asked impatiently. "For Pete's sake, tell me!"

The little man leaned closer to Marc's ear. "Common spirits!" he hissed importantly. "Whiskey!"

"No!" Marc was incredulous. "You must have made some mist...!"

"Here, here," Agatha said, making impatient motions with her gun. "No loitering. I'm really not going to speak to you again."

"That's a break," Marc said.

He and Mr. Culpepper started forward and as they passed the inverted crate in the center of the room Marc dropped momentarily behind. When he emerged a moment later a rather singular bulge had appeared in the region of his shirt front, and he was clutching his stomach.

"What's the matter with you?" Agatha asked wearily.

"Bellyache," Marc announced flatly, struggling past her. "You make me sick at my stomach."

Agatha's expression became pained. "Vile little boy," she murmured.

It was dark when the delivery truck nosed out of the alley and headed back toward the city. Having locked the doors to the rear compartment from the outside, Agatha had taken her place beside Chadwick in the front, her pistol draped elegantly over her shoulder. She had been keeping a sharp eye trained toward the compartment, but it was too dark back there for her to see much. Her charges, however, seemed disinclined toward revolt. In fact, as the trip wore on, they appeared to become positively hilarious about the whole thing. Soft tittering occasionally issued from the darkness, sometimes interlaced with boisterous guffaws. Agatha wondered about this but didn't discover the reason for it until the truck reached its destination and pulled to a stop in the parking lot behind Marc's office building. When she unlocked the doors and reopened them, Marc, Toffee and Mr. Culpepper peered out at her owlishly, swaying together in silent harmony.

"Good ol' Aggie," Marc giggled, dropping his appropriated bottle shatteringly at the woman's feet. "Long may she rave."

"Well, I'll be!" Agatha murmured. "They're drunk as skunks, the lot of them."

"Eh?" Chadwick inquired, moving to her side. "Who's drunk?"

"The tykes," Agatha said, "and the old man. They're lubricated, you might say, like a lawn mower in May."

Chadwick peered inside, gazed unbelievingly at the swaying trio. He wagged a finger. "Shame," he said. He reached inside and lifted Toffee out.

Made forgetful of her transformation by her recent libations, Toffee twined her arms around Chadwick's neck.

"Hello, handsome," she cooed throatily.

"Put her down," Agatha snapped. "There's something not quite right about that child. I don't like the funny way she's looking at you. I won't stand for it."

Apparently Chadwick, too, had noticed something a bit unusual about the infant in his arms, but was not entirely displeased. He smiled confusedly. "She's only a youngster," he said.

"I don't care," Agatha retorted. "Youngster or not, no female is going to look at you like that and get away with it. Why, even at twenty I hadn't a gleam in my eye like that."

"Oh, I wouldn't say that, my dear," Chadwick said. "I remember a night when you were only eighteen...."

"Enough!" Agatha commanded with agitation. "There's something improper about that child and you're to put her down this instant. I shudder to think what she'll be like when she grows up. If she ever does, that is."

At this juncture Mr. Culpepper hopped out of the truck, teetered precariously on one foot for a moment, and sprawled out on the ground. Propping his head up on one elbow, he gazed up at Agatha, a new boldness in his eye. He winked debonairly.

"Hi, yuh, toots," he gurgled.

Agatha appeared to have bitten into a sour apple. "Ugh!" she said. "How depraved!"

Except for occasional dim lights on the stair landings the office building was completely dark. The labored progress of the strange party wending its way to the fourth floor was accompanied by a fruity assortment of stumblings, curses and giggles. When they finally arrived at the offices of the Pillsworth Advertising Agency, Marc handed his keys to Mr. Culpepper under the false impression that the little man could better negotiate the keyhole. To the befogged scientist, however, the lock was a writhing, squirming thing that constantly and with utter perverseness, avoided his grasp. The struggle became a very personal thing with the little man. He threw himself against the door with all his might.

"Won't hold still, eh?" he challenged. "Well, we'll see about that!"

With a snort of disgust, Agatha took the keys from the little man, shoved him aside, and opened the door. With a curt nod she directed the others inside.

The journey through the outer office was accomplished without mishap, though Mr. Culpepper, running afoul of a swivel chair, had to be restrained from attacking the whirling piece of furniture bodily. Marc and Toffee took him in charge and guided him gently into Marc's private office, where Agatha and Chadwick had preceded them and turned on the lights.

Agatha turned on Toffee threateningly. "Well, we're here," she said. "Where are the pills?"

Toffee nodded toward the desk. "Over there," she said. "The green bottle."

At the sight of the bottle both Agatha and Chadwick seemed to lose a good deal of their dignified reserve; they fairly trampled each other in a rush for the desk. Reaching the bottle, they grappled openly across the desk for its possession. Marc and Toffee dropped Mr. Culpepper to the lounge and stood by for developments.

"Give it here!" Agatha shrilled. "Let me have it, do you hear!"

"I'll let you have it right enough," Chadwick grunted back at her. "I'll let you have it right in the eye with my fist."

"Louse!" Agatha yelled. "I'm going to be head of this organization. I have the brains anyway."

"Since when?" Chadwick jeered. "If it weren't for me you'd still be carrying grog behind a bar."

"Yes," Agatha said evilly, trying to twist the bottle out of his hand, "and you, sponge that you are, would be soaking it up as fast as I could carry it. Give me that bottle, you old rummy."

"Take your grasping claws off it," Chadwick said levelly, "before I lose my temper. I'll see that the pills are handled properly."

"Properly for whom?" Agatha rasped. "You'd hog them all for yourself, that's what you'd do!"

Both of them stood their ground. The struggle was apparently one to the finish; obviously whichever of them emerged the victor would be in control of the other forever after. Deep within them primitive instincts had been set to work to choose the chieftain ... or chieftainess, as the case might be ... of their proposed "organization." As the contest left the field of invective and entered onto the more taxing one of physical, brute force, they both seemed to forget their captives. Dropping their guns to the floor, first Agatha, then Chadwick, they shoved their free hands in each other's faces and began to push. At this, Marc and Toffee, with a little cry of triumph, acted as a team in swooping away from the lounge and retrieving the guns from the floor.

Looking somewhat like an infant Annie Oakley, Toffee stepped back, aimed her pistol in the general direction of the battling Harpers and shouted, "Stick 'em up!"

But the Harpers had other things on their minds. Chadwick had just let out an enraged bellow as Agatha's even, white teeth had bitten into one of his fingers.

Toffee looked helplessly at Marc. "What'll we do?" she asked.

Marc was already doing it. Aiming at the ceiling, he brought a shower of plaster thunderously down over the scene of the battle. The Harpers instantly became transfixed, a frozen study of hand-to-hand combat. Leaning over the table, their faces almost together, they stared fixedly at each other through a screen of fingers. They had the look of people suddenly remembering something very important.

"Hands up!" Toffee piped.

The Harpers came to life in the same moment and reacted with their customary single-mindedness. Two pairs of hands shot into the air, and as a result the bottle crashed to the top of the desk, pills rolling in all directions. The desk and portions of the floor around the desk seemed to have been the scene of a recent snowstorm.

"I'll keep them covered," Toffee told Marc. "You get the police."

"The police?" Marc said. "How will we explain who they are? With their new faces, I mean. For that matter, how will we explain who *we* are? The cops are looking for us, too, you know."

"I see what you mean," Toffee said thoughtfully. "It's rather an impasse, isn't it?" She turned to Mr. Culpepper who, roused by the sound of the shot, was now weaving his way toward them. "What about that antidote?" she asked him. "If whiskey's supposed to restore us, heaven knows we've had whiskey aplenty."

"Takes time," the little man said thickly. "Mustn't expect miracles, you know."

"Oh, mustn't I?" Toffee said with sudden heat. "You change me into a miserable little blob of flab and then you have the gall to tell me not to expect miracles. That's a laugh ... a fair howl."

The little man chuckled. "It is rather humorous, isn't it?" he said.

"I ought to kick in your bridgework," Toffee said dully.

"You don't like me," Mr. Culpepper said with no particular expression. "You think I'm disgusting."

"You think you're kidding," Toffee said. "You've just shown real insight."

"Thank you," the little man said gravely. "Sometimes I think...."

In a start of surprise he lurched to one side, grasping a chair for support. His eyes, like Agatha's and Chadwick's, were fastened on Marc and Toffee. Suddenly, the two erstwhile youngsters had begun to stretch upward like a pair of extending telescopes. They were growing and aging with the speed of lightning, it seemed. In a matter of seconds Marc became once again a tall, serious-eyed businessman ... one that had unaccountably rolled up his trousers to go wading. At his side Toffee was again a scantily clad redhead ... a fine figure of a girl with a fine figure. The effect was impressive to say the least. The Harpers gasped in unison.

Toffee stretched out one of her exquisite legs and surveyed it with satisfaction. "Well, that's more like it," she said happily. "A girl can really get places with a pair of pins like that."

"I told you!" Agatha shrieked. "I told you there was something funny about her. Only it isn't funny!"

"Oh, Lord," Chadwick murmured. "I've never seen anything so weird in all my life. How did they manage it?"

"Don't ask me," Agatha said unhappily. "I don't like to even think about it."

Marc had also stretched out a leg, but the sight of it seemed to give him no particular pleasure. Hastily, still holding his gun on Agatha and Chadwick, he reached out and rolled down his trousers.

"Well, thank heaven that's over," he sighed. "What a relief."

"Hypnosis," Chadwick said to Agatha. "That's what it is. Either they hypnotized us into thinking they were children a while ago, or they're hypnotizing us now to make us think they're adults. I wonder which they really are?"

"I don't care," Agatha said with sudden disillusion. "I don't care if they're really a pair of Newfoundland puppies. I don't care about anything anymore."

"I told you," Mr. Culpepper said to Toffee. "It worked like a charm. Now you don't have to be sore at me any more."

Toffee favored the little man with a radiant smile. "I could kiss you," she said recklessly.

"Please do," Mr. Culpepper said.

"Later," Toffee said. "Much later." She turned to Marc. "The decks are clear. Call the cops. Let's get rid of these regal rats."

Marc nodded and retired to the telephone. "We can say they broke in here," he said, "if all else fails."

Toffee, in the meantime, had leveled her gun on the Harpers. "Turn-about is some fun, eh, kids?" she said. "And while we're waiting for the cops, why don't you tell us what really happened to the Duchess of Windsor's jewels? Remember, anything you say will be used to hang you."

Mr. Culpepper teetered to Toffee's side. Screwing his face into what he fondly believed to be a romantic pucker, he lifted himself to his toes and growled, "Kiss me, baby," a la Clark Gable. He wavered a moment and then fell forward.

It might have been the perverse paw of destiny that sent the little man crashing against Toffee. Otherwise, the situation involving the Harpers, Mr. Culpepper and Fixage might easily have righted itself on the spot. The Harpers might have been carted off to the pokey in chains; Mr. Culpepper might have returned to his laboratory for a late pot of coffee; Fixage might have become an unpleasant memory, and Marc and Toffee might have been free to disport themselves in any way that pleased them. It might have happened that way. But it didn't.

Under Mr. Culpepper's sudden weight Toffee tottered a moment, then crumpled to the floor, dropping her gun. She showed splendid presence of mind in retrieving the gun swiftly enough to ward off any attack from the Harpers. But she wasn't quick enough to prevent the enterprising twosome from scooping up handfuls of the scattered pills and greedily popping them into their mouths.

"Don't!" Toffee screamed, leaping to her feet. "Spit them out!"

Agatha swallowed mightily and gasped for air. She laughed shortly. "Too late now," she said triumphantly.

"You've no idea," Toffee said. "If you did, you'd be courting a stomach pump with everything that's in you."

Marc slapped the telephone receiver back into place. "Good night," he murmured, aghast. "Whole handfuls of the things!"

Chadwick managed to choke down his generous grabbings. "Well," he said with satisfaction, "now we'll see what's what."

"And probably a good deal more," Toffee said. "If we can bear to look." She glanced down at Mr. Culpepper who was still resting quietly on the floor. "What can we do about it?"

The little man shrugged, uninterested. "You cheated," he mumbled. "You ducked."

"We ought to do something right away," Marc put in. "Maybe a stomach pump isn't such a bad idea. In a minute it'll be too late. There's a...."

It was already too late.

The Harpers had suddenly turned an unfortunate shade of whitish-green. They clutched at each other in a paroxysm of agony, shuddering from head to toe. Then, seized by a rending spasm that nearly doubled them, they slid soundlessly to the floor.

"Oh, Chad...!" Agatha whimpered. Her head fell loosely to the pit of Chadwick's stomach. "Ohhhh!" And then she passed out.

Chadwick was unmoved by his mate's pitiful lamentations; he had been dead to the world even before he touched the floor.

Toffee regarded the crumpled figures at her feet. "How terrible!" she breathed. "Do you suppose they're dead?"

Marc shook his head. "They're still breathing," he said.

Mr. Culpepper, after a number of false starts, finally made it to his feet. His eyes wandered loosely about the room for a time, and finally arrived at the bodies on the floor.

"With all their fine manners," he mused, "you'd think they'd find a more suitable place to retire."

"Oh, shut up," Marc sighed. "If you don't I may cram a few of those pills down your gullet."

Agatha and Chadwick remained in their state of enforced slumber only a few minutes. Then, almost at the same time, they awoke and opened their eyes. Chadwick glanced dazedly around, stretched luxuriously and yawned a cavernous yawn. Agatha, however, seemed to suffer no after effects at all. She merely opened her eyes, surveyed the situation briefly and went directly to the business at hand. Getting to her feet, she regarded Marc and Toffee triumphantly.

"Well," she sneered, "now we'll see about that turn-about stuff. You needn't try to scare us with those guns any longer, either." She turned and helped Chadwick to his feet.

"What happened?" Chadwick asked. "What hit me?"

"The pills," Agatha reminded him. "We're all set, love. We've nothing more to worry about. Shall we quit this dreadful place?"

"Oh, yes," Chadwick smiled. "We did take the pills, didn't we? We're bullet-proof. To coin an expression, the world is practically ours."

Agatha took him by the arm. "Yes, dear," she said gaily. "Tax free, too. Shall we duck out and rifle a few banks just for a starter?" her voice was exuberant, almost giddy.

"Right-ho," Chadwick said agreeably. "And maybe a jewelry shop or two, eh? Just for good luck."

They started happily toward the door, too wrapped up in their gold-tinted dreams of the future to notice the fascinated, expectant gaze of their erstwhile adversaries. They were almost into the outer office when it happened. Unquestionably it was the shock of their lives.

They seemed to melt like popsicles in a furnace. They dwindled so swiftly there was the faint sound of disturbed atmosphere, a little rush of air. Suddenly their clothes were hanging loosely about them, the ends of their sleeves trailing on the floor. And they were still melting. Agatha screamed with terror; and even as she did her voice faded away into a thin, childish wail.

"Oh, heavens!" Toffee cried. "They took too much. They're disappearing entirely!" She buried her face against Marc's shoulder. "I can't look!"

Marc and Mr. Culpepper stared at the spectacle with open-mouthed amazement.

It was a long time before Toffee found the courage to turn away from Marc's shoulder. When she did, her eyes moved apprehensively toward the door, and then she made a little whimpering sound. Two forlorn little piles of clothing lay there, one on either side of the doorway.

"Ohhh, Lord," Toffee breathed. "They're gone ... completely gone. There's nothing left of them, not even a whisper."

"'Fraid you're right," Marc said. "Fixage fixed 'em."

Mr. Culpepper had been greatly sobered by the disappearance of the Harpers. "I had no idea," he muttered woodenly. "No idea at all."

"I feel sorry," Toffee said. "I can't help it. They were so proud and so elegant ... even if they were just a couple of rats."

"*Rats indeed!*"

Toffee started as though slapped in the nether regions with a cactus. The voice had been nothing more than a tiny whine, a mere vibration, but it had seemed to come from the heap of clothing that had been Agatha's. Toffee streaked across the room and knelt beside the crumpled garments. They seemed furiously agitated.

With deft fingers Toffee dug inside the clothing. First she uncovered a tiny, wrinkled hand, then an arm and finally an entire baby. The infant was very red of face and its small features were screwed up into an expression of extreme annoyance. Its button eyes blazed malevolently as it gazed at Toffee. It gritted its tiny teeth.

"Witch!" it hissed. "Oh, the things I would call you if I weren't a lady."

"Agatha!" Toffee cried. She lowered the infant back onto the pile of clothing and turned to the tangle of male garments on the other side of the door.

A brief search through a coat, a shirt and an undershirt uncovered Chadwick, also in an acute state of infancy. When he looked up and saw Toffee staring down at him he blushed furiously.

"Give me my trousers!" the baby demanded hotly. "Stop staring at me and give me my trousers!"

"Well, for heaven sake!" Toffee exclaimed.

She placed the depleted Harpers side by side on the lounge, and Marc and Mr. Culpepper moved to her side. As babies, the erstwhile thieves were markedly unbeautiful, and Toffee musingly remarked as much. At this the infant Agatha surprisingly forgot herself and poured out a string of oaths such as would have done credit to a stevedore on a hot day. Chadwick continued to blush.

"What are we going to do with them?" Toffee asked. "We can't turn them over to the police like this."

"Certainly not," Marc agreed. "And we can't keep them around. If my wife should suddenly come home and find me with a couple of babies...." He shuddered at the thought. "We'll have to restore them." He turned to Mr. Culpepper. "We can do that, can't we?"

"Yes!" Toffee cried. "We could bring them back to what they were before their faces were changed, couldn't we? That would solve everything."

This suggestion provoked a discordant howl from the infant Harpers.

"I don't know," the little scientist mused. "It could be done all right, but it would have to be done very carefully. We'd have to give them spirits in exact amounts. A little too much one way or another...." He stroked the tip of his nose with a slender finger. "Figuring on the basis of the amounts that you and Mr. Pillsworth consumed to restore yourselves, I could probably...." He retreated to the chair behind Marc's desk, tilted his head back and closed his eyes. "Yes, yes," he murmured dreamily.

"Will you just listen!" Agatha piped. "They're going to work us out a whiskey formula."

"I don't care what they work out," Chadwick replied, rolling unhappily over onto his fat little stomach. "I want some clothes. I'm cold and embarrassed."

"See if you can find something for them to wear," Marc said, turning to Toffee. "Try the model's dressing rooms in the photographer's studio; there may be something there." He glanced briefly at Toffee's faintly obscured figure. "And while you're about it," he added, "you might pick up something for yourself."

Toffee nodded and left the room. When she returned she was resplendent in a shimmering ice-blue evening gown that had a very conservative neckline ... provided a girl's neck, by some freak of nature, commenced somewhere in the region of her midriff. The glistening material clung tightly to her body, highlighting its more provocative features. When she walked she shimmered with a loveliness that seemed almost unreal.

In her hand she was carrying two brief lengths of black velvet. These she twined haphazardly around the rather brief figures of Agatha and Chadwick.

"How's that little wretch coming with our formula?" Agatha asked.

"Yes," Chadwick put in, "I could do with a spot or two very nicely just now."

Toffee glanced at Mr. Culpepper who, for all the world, seemed merely to be enjoying a sound sleep. His facial muscles twitched occasionally, though, giving testimony to the experimental processes that were being accomplished inside.

"Keep your diapers on," Toffee said. "He's doing what he can."

"Oh, well," Chadwick sighed. "I suppose there's really no hurry. They'll only turn us over to the police when we're restored."

"I don't care," Agatha said, eyeing Toffee's new loveliness with envy. "I'd rather rot in jail than be left to go on groveling around like this."

There was a sudden snort from Mr. Culpepper as his head snapped forward, and his eyes opened. "I have it," he announced composedly. "As I have it figured, ten jiggers of strong whiskey should restore them to what they were six months ago." He turned to Marc. "Do you have any liquor handy?"

Marc shook his head. "We'll have to go out for it."

"Very well," Mr. Culpepper said. "I'll go."

"No. We'll all have to go," Marc said. "We can't risk staying here. The cleaning ladies will be around this way soon. If they saw this ..." he indicated the babies and Toffee, "... there would be a scandal that would make Hollywood furious with envy."

Leaving the building, the Pillsworth party was one to startle and confound, a woman in a revealing evening gown carrying two velvet-swathed babies and accompanied by two extremely uneasy looking gentlemen, was a sight to give pause to even the most careless-minded citizen. Indeed, several citizens not only paused but stopped cold in their tracks as they saw the strange group moving toward them. With grave dignity, though, glancing neither to the right nor to the left, the ill-matched fivesome proceeded to the end of the block, waited in heavy silence for a change of traffic signals, crossed the street and disappeared through the doors of a retail liquor store. There they were greeted by a large, befuddled looking merchant.

The merchant surveyed his approaching customers with silent disbelief. Then he seemed to shake himself from an absorbing dream.

"This is a liquor store," he said dully.

"Yes, we know," Toffee said politely. "That's why we've come."

"I just thought I'd mention it," the merchant said unhappily, clearing his throat. He glanced out the window and closed his eyes a minute. Then he turned back to the group before the counter and seemed to be surprised all over again.

"Since you're really here," he said, "what can I do for you?"

"We'd like a bottle of strong whiskey," Toffee said. She turned questioningly to Mr. Culpepper who nodded back to her approvingly. "The strongest you have."

"Two bottles!" a tiny voice suddenly piped from the depths of one of the velvet bundles. Chadwick's small head bobbed into sight. "Make it two! And make it snappy!"

Agatha's head was only a moment behind Chadwick's in making its appearance, "Sot!" she accused. "Greedy little pig!"

"You be still," Chadwick rejoined. "What if I do get a little drunk tonight? Who ever had a better reason? Just being married to you would be enough, I should think! I've got it coming to me."

"You've got a lot coming to you," Agatha shrilled. "And someday you're going to get it. If it hadn't been for you starting that fight up there...."

"Please," the infant Chadwick said, looking pained. "Try to restrain your shrewish tendencies just this once, won't you?" He turned to the liquor merchant with a bland smile. "Two bottles, if you please, friend."

"Yes," Toffee put in quickly, by way of ending the discussion. "Two bottles, if you please."

"Perhaps it's just as well," Agatha drawled. "I wouldn't drink from the same bottle with that little lush, anyway."

The merchant made a brief, strangling noise as he tore his eyes away from Agatha and Chadwick and backed into a shelf, upsetting several bottles onto the floor. "I shouldn't of nipped the stock in the back room," he muttered to himself. "Me old lady warned me this would happen. She said it would start just this way." He turned his back on Toffee and the infants, grasped the edge of the shelf and rested his head on the backs of his hands. A deep shudder ran the full length of his body. It was some time before he began to recover even a little bit.

Finally, without turning around, he managed to say, "What kind of whiskey did you want, lady?"

Toffee looked at Agatha and Chadwick questioningly.

"What kind have you got?" Agatha called out.

The merchant shuddered again. "I don't know," he whimpered. "I don't know nuthin' right now. Maybe this is all Chanel number 5 up here on these shelves. It wouldn't surprise me none. Why don't you just look around and take what you want? I won't look. You just take it and go away. Just tip-toe out and don't slam the door. That's all I ask. The liquor is on the house."

After the selection of two large, rather vaporish-looking bottles, the little company returned to the sidewalk. The babies, however, were becoming increasingly troublesome in their eagerness to be at the liquor, which was in Marc's custody for the time being. Their ill-tempered cries, however, were almost entirely directed at Toffee. People began to stop in the streets to watch and to listen. If they could believe their ears, they were overhearing two new-born infants calling their mother names that even an adult hadn't any right to know. Shocking invective gushed from the sweet mouths of the babes in a fountainous stream. Toffee, probably for the first time in her life, was embarrassed.

"Can't we do something?" she asked her companion. "Can't we go somewhere? If this sort of thing goes on much longer I'll be picked up by a home for wayward mothers or something."

Marc glanced down the street. Then he pointed. "Over there," he said. His finger indicated a public library. "There should be quiet and privacy in there." He turned to the babies. "Now listen here, you two, either you be quiet and behave yourselves or you won't get a drop. Understand?"

Agatha and Chadwick were instantly subdued.

The library was a large, high-ceilinged place of passages and corridors. Just inside the main entrance was a large foyer-like room out of the center of which, like a giant mushroom, jutted a circular checking counter. Toffee moved quickly to the counter and rested the babies on it. An aged woman whose spinsterish face belied her gay dress turned and smiled, revealing a mouth full of charred fags.

"Yes?" she asked.

"Where are the books?" Toffee asked.

"What books?"

Toffee looked puzzled for a moment. "Big books," she said. "In stacks. I was told there were veritable walls of books in here."

"And there are," the woman said defensively. "Which books are you interested in?"

"How should I know?" Toffee asked helplessly. "I haven't read them yet."

The woman sighed. Then her eyes fell to Agatha and Chadwick lying on the counter and they lighted with the fanatical gleam of frustrated motherhood. She reached out and pulled back the velvet folds.

"My, what beaut...!" The lie died in her throat. To suggest that Agatha and Chadwick were anything but downright ugly was too great a falsehood for even this child-starved soul. "You must be ... uh ... proud," she said tonelessly. However, she was game; once she'd started she wasn't going to give up. She reached out a hand and waggled a finger over Agatha's protruding tummy.

"Kitchy-kitchy," she said unhappily.

Anger flashed in the infant's eyes. "Get your horny talons off me, you withered old wraith," she snapped. And having given warning, she parted her bubbling lips and bit the woman's finger.

The woman didn't cry out in surprise; she didn't make any sound at all. She simply stared hard at Toffee for a long moment, then silently pointed to a distant corridor.

"The books on abnormal child psychology are in there," she whispered. "And if I were you, honey, I'd hurry."

Toffee gathered up Agatha and Chadwick and joined Marc and Mr. Culpepper, who had been watching from a distance.

"That was fine," she scolded Agatha. "That was a splendid display."

"What did you expect?" Agatha replied haughtily. "The old hag was thumbing me like a ripe watermelon."

"I wish she'd throttled you," Toffee said annoyedly. "Lord knows you deserve it. Your mothers must have been women of great forbearance. How they kept their hands off your little throats is more than I can tell."

The little party made its way through the nearest passage and found itself in a forest of books. Shelves lined on either side stretched out toward them like great, reaching fingers. Here and there a solitary "browser" was picking his way painfully along the long rows, title by title, but on the whole the great, book-jammed room was reasonably deserted. Toffee moved along the ends of the rows, found a browserless section and disappeared inside. Marc and Mr. Culpepper followed. Together, they all retreated to the end of the section and formed a sort of huddle. Marc produced the bottles from beneath his coat.

"How are we going to measure it?" Toffee asked. "We have to give them ten jiggers exactly."

"Do I have to think of everything?" Agatha inquired scornfully. Her small hand emerged from her velvet wrappings, clutching a jigger glass. "It was lying around loose on the counter," she explained.

"As in womanhood," Toffee said philosophically, "so, too, in infancy is she a crook."

As though in solemn ritual, the bottles were silently opened and the initial portion poured.

Agatha stretched out her miniature hand. "Gimme," she said. "It's my glass. And, boy, do I need a slug!"

"Tell me, dear," Toffee said quietly, tilting the glass to Agatha's eager mouth, "whatever became of that lovely accent of yours?"

Agatha polished off the whiskey and burped. "None of your damned business," she said with truly childish simplicity.

By alternating between the two babes, a certain amount of decorum was maintained. Marc took charge of the stoking of Chadwick while Toffee continued in behalf of Agatha. Mr. Culpepper shoved a few volumes aside on one of the lower shelves and seated himself, watching with interest as the glass moved from hand to hand to bottle to baby. He looked like a spectator at a tennis game being played on a checker board. The glass shuttled from pouted lip to pouted lip until the inner infant, on both scores, had been fortified five times over. From this point on, as the whiskey poured down the tiny throats, a corresponding amount of exuberance arose via the same channel. Agatha, made congenial by the liquor, began to while away the time between drinks by lifting her childish voice in song.

"Becky lived in a Turkish harem," she chortled. "She had towels but she wouldn't wear 'em."

"Stop that caterwauling," Toffee commanded.

Agatha perversely increased her volume. "Becky looked like Theda Barer," she shrieked. "Theda was bare but Becky was barer!"

Suddenly a sharp, gasping sound echoed around the little group, seeming to come from no place in particular; the bookshelves themselves appeared to be making little twittering sounds of surprise. The Pillsworth party froze as it was. Eyes moved furtively in unturning heads. It was Toffee who discovered the cause of the interruption.

Several books had been removed from one of the upper shelves, leaving a sort of peep hole into the next section. In this opening had appeared the forbidding face of the spinsterish librarian. It bore the dismayed expression of a maiden lady who had inadvertently stumbled into a YMCA swimming pool.

"Heavens!" the woman gasped. "Giving liquor to *babies*! No wonder they're retarded!"

Toffee, recognizing the situation for what it was, displayed what she believed was great presence of mind in grabbing the tell-tale bottle from the shelf and lifting it to her own lips. She drank deeply of the contents, and just to lend conviction to her performance as a ravening drunkard, staggered against the bookshelves, rolling her eyes loosely in their sockets.

"Oh, dear," Mr. Culpepper put in from the perch on the shelf. "If I were you, I don't think I'd...."

A little moan issued from the colorless face in the bookshelf. "Oooo, what depravity!" it exclaimed. "And teaching the babies to drink, too!"

"Nonsense," Toffee said, addressing the face openly. "We're drinking this ourselves. We're just a bunch of roaring sots. We're too stingy to give any to the babies."

"I saw you," the face insisted. "You were forcing the filthy stuff on those infants. You ought to be reported."

Toffee turned to Marc. "We weren't either, were we?" she asked. "We never give these babies any liquor, do we?"

"Certainly not," Marc said indignantly. "We were only fighting them off, trying to keep them from taking it away from us. We love the stuff too much to waste it on them."

In demonstration, he grabbed the bottle that had been Chadwick's and pressed it eagerly to his mouth, a fanatical gleam in his eye.

"Oh, really," Mr. Culpepper cried. "I really don't think...."

"You see," Toffee said to the face. "Can't leave the stuff alone. Those babies haven't got a look-in as far as liquor is concerned. We wouldn't give them a drop if they were dying of thirst."

Doubt came into the face as Marc withdrew the bottle from his lips with a loud smacking noise and grandly wiped his mouth with the back of his hand. The librarian was beginning to look more or less convinced. Slowly, the face started to move away.

"Becky's boy friend came and found her," Agatha suddenly shrilled in a voice that was definitely dewy. "But her towels were not...."

The voice suddenly became softly muffled, as though by velvet.

The face darted back into the opening between the books. "What was that?" it asked.

"Me," Toffee said. "I like music with my liquor."

The face was some reassured. "Well, you'll have to stop it," it snapped. "You'll have to stop almost everything you're doing, in fact, if you expect to remain here. Drinking is not allowed...."

A loud, rumbling burp issued from the velvet bundle in Toffee's arms.

"Oh!" the face exclaimed, and suddenly disappeared. There was the sound of quick tapping footsteps on the other side of the shelf.

When the footsteps had died away Toffee and Marc, with renewed vigor, returned to their labors with the bottles and the babies.

"We'll have to hurry," Marc said. "That old hag had a look about her that definitely meant trouble if you ask me."

"I agree," Toffee said. She glanced down at Agatha. "And you didn't help matters any. You displayed your customary perverseness, I noticed."

The baby cocked an insolent eye at her. "You acted with rare intelligence, yourself," she said. "In my opinion you handled the situation like a jerk. I only shudder that all these strangers are laboring under the degrading notion that you are my mother."

The liquor flowed with increasing velocity. The eighth jigger had been administered when the footsteps sounded in the doorway beyond the book shelves. They entered the room and hurried forward as though they knew just where they were going.

"In there!" came the voice of the aging librarian. "They're in section five, throwing a regular wild party! They're drinking liquor and singing dirty songs and ... and ... contributing to the delinquency of babies! They're carrying on 'till you wouldn't believe it!"

"My!" a voice said, not untinged with pleased expectancy. "Sounds like the time we raided that house over on the other side...."

"Shut up," another voice said. "No matter what's goin' on behind them books, this is different. And don't you forget it!"

The footsteps drew closer and swiftly rounded the end of the section. The members of the Pillsworth party looked up in unison and saw two large, blue-clad policemen running toward them.

Toffee fairly threw Agatha into the arms of Mr. Culpepper. "Here!" she said. "I'll hold them off. You see that she gets the other two shots!" She sounded like the little Dutch boy about to cram his pinky into that dyke over in Holland. Agatha landed in Mr. Culpepper's lap with a thud and a burp.

Thus relieved of her besotted burden Toffee raced quickly to a movable ladder stretched up against the long shelves. Reaching it, she started upward, two rungs at a time.

The ladder was the sort that rested on rollers at either end and could easily be shuttled from one location to another with a good deal of facility. Once aloft Toffee lost no time in using the contrivance to its utmost capacity. Rollers whirred and Toffee and the ladder sped forward to the attack, toward a section that was notable for the number of truly weighty volumes it housed. Toffee seized up the first of these volumes and paused momentarily to read its title.

"War and Peace," she read. "That ought to put them to sleep."

Never was literature so forced upon anyone as it was on the hapless policemen in the awful moments that followed. "War and Peace," true to Toffee's expectations did indeed leave the first of the cops looking extremely drowsy as it clipped him on the chin and sent him staggering backwards against his companion. In a matter of seconds two of the city's finest were groveling pitifully on the floor, trying vainly to ward off a hail storm of books. Toffee, in selecting a lettered diet for these two besieged gentlemen showed a marked preference for the heavier works. Her victims were most impressed, in a very physical sort of way, with the works of the ancient Greeks.

The cops, apparently unwilling to perish under this literary avalanche, turned tail, and started crawling toward the outer protection of the shelves. Seeing that victory ... at least momentary victory ... was at hand, Toffee turned back to see what progress was being made with the howling Harpers. Everything at the end of the section was oddly serene.

Agatha had been set aside on one of the shelves and apparently the last of the ten libations was being given to Chadwick. While Toffee was watching this picture of rather distorted domestic contentment, one of the cops timidly extended his head around the lower corner of one of the shelves.

"Lord," he commented to his companion, "they're choking whiskey down them young'uns like it was a matter of life and death. What do you suppose they wanna do that for?"

"Maybe they get a kick out of drunk babies," the other returned morosely. "Maybe hooched-up babies are a barrel of fun. How should I know?"

"Looks more like they're tryin' to kill 'em," said the peeping cop. "Infanticide is a serious charge. Attempted infanticide is just as bad. It's goin' to go hard on 'em when we get 'em outa there."

"*If* we get 'em outa there," his companion corrected. "Me, I feel almost like just crawlin' outa here and lettin' 'em do as they please."

"Shame on you, Murphy," the first cop said. "It's our duty to protect them babies, even if they don't look very human."

"What'll we do?"

The cop surveyed the situation; Toffee was now facing away from them, watching as Chadwick was being shelved beside Agatha.

"Now's our chance," he said. "Let's rush 'em."

"I wouldn't mind rushin' that redhead," Murphy said stoutly, "if I could just get out of the readin' room. She flings a mean book."

"Let's go," the first cop whispered. "No time to jaw."

Together, the policemen rushed once more onto the scene of their recent defeat. Somehow confused, they both ran headlong for Toffee and the ladder. Apparently neither remembered the swift mobility of the ladder for, simultaneously, they lunged at it, throwing their full weight against it.

Instantly the ladder shot into motion, fully burdened with the two startled cops and a thoroughly unbalanced Toffee. At the outset Toffee toppled from her perch, hurtled downward, and caught one of the cops around the neck just in time to prevent a crashing arrival at the floor. From there on, it was just one grand, piggy-back ride for the redhead. For the cop it was a matter of an extra burden and hanging on for dear life. Books, row upon row of them, flashed by in a screaming blur. They were heading for a dead end with the speed of a bullet.

"Get off me!" Toffee's protector yelled ungallantly. "Beat it, lady! No riders!"

"Not on your life!" Toffee hollered back through clenched teeth. "For the rest of this trip you and I are sweethearts!"

At this moment the librarian appeared at the end of the book littered aisle and gazed on the scene within with open amazement. "Just look at those cops!" she exclaimed. "Carrying on just as bad as the others! You'd think this was a fun house. You boys stop that this instant!" she yelled. "I'm going to call the commissioner!"

"When you do, lady," one of the policemen hollered back, "tell him for me what he can do with his lousy job! I got a wife and kids to think of!"

Just then, the ladder, like a transcontinental express, arrived at the end of the line and discharged its protesting passengers like three jet propelled missiles. The two policemen shot out into the air, headed directly for Marc and Mr. Culpepper who had been watching the little excursion in a state of rigid immobility. Toffee, through some hitherto undiscovered law of physics, left the back of her stalwart carrier in a sweeping upward arc that landed her ungently atop the book shelves.

The law literally swept down on Marc and Mr. Culpepper, upending them posthaste and hurling them to the floor. From the top of the bookcase, Toffee collected her breath and gazed blandly on the scene of confusion below. She might have hurled a book or two in Marc's behalf, except that in the tangle of arms and legs, it was impossible to tell which were the property of Marc. Besides, she had just become happily aware of a window at her side, one that was easily accessible from the top of the book shelves. She threw the catch and it slid open.

Turning her attention back to the confusion on the floor, she was delighted to see that Marc and Mr. Culpepper had emerged from the "flail" and were dazedly looking about for some new, less hazardous enterprise.

"Up here!" Toffee yelled, pointing to the window. "Up the ladder!"

They reacted mechanically. They gazed dully at Toffee and the window, then started obediently toward the ladder. They were nearly to the top of the shelves when the two cops, finally weary of struggling with each other on the floor, got to their feet and observed these recent developments with considerable malice.

"Oh, no you don't!" one of them grated viciously. He lunged at the ladder and shoved it with all his might. As it shot away from his hand he let out a hysterical laugh. "There!" he yelled. "Now it's your turn to look silly!"

The ladder streaked away toward the open end of the section like a shrieking, avenging thing. Marc and Mr. Culpepper twined themselves to it and each other in a seizure of iron-bound desperation.

"Heh, heh, heh!" the cop cackled wildly, watching their terror. "That'll teach 'em to make light of the law!" He turned his attention to Toffee. "Come down off there, you little witch," he demanded.

"Come and get me, lardhead," Toffee hissed. "I'm holding out for squatter's rights."

Toffee smiled enticingly from her perch on top of the bookcase as the cop gestured wildly....

The cop accepted her invitation. Or at least he tried. Clutching the edge of a high shelf he attempted to swing himself upward. From there on, the natural laws of gravity took matters into their own hands. The entire bookcase teetered drunkenly for a moment, swayed forward, paused, then clattered downward. Toffee's pursuer went down under a flood of literature, while Toffee sailed lightly outward and landed with ease in the outstretched arms of the other policeman. All three of the participants in this rather singular incident were starkly surprised at its outcome.

At the same moment a howling duet of horror announced the arrival of Marc and Mr. Culpepper at their dreaded destination. There was a thud and a crash as the ladder hit the end of its track and hurled its helpless cargo into the wall. A clatter, a moan and a groan marked the end of the operation.

"Now look what you've done!" Toffee howled as the cop lowered her to the floor. "You've probably killed them!"

A howl of outrage issued from the mountain of books at her side. A few slid from the top of the pile and the head of the deluged policeman jutted into view, eyes ablaze. "You haven't increased my insurance value either, sister," he said bitterly. He burrowed his way to freedom and gained his feet, staring evilly at the diminutive cause of his downfall. "I—hate—you," he said with heavy emphasis.

By the time Toffee and the cops arrived at the end of the section, Marc and Mr. Culpepper were just beginning to stir. Apparently their nervous systems had suffered the bulk of the damage, for they were not noticeably marked. The cops took them into hand.

"Fun's over boys!" the more unruffled of them said. "You won't go sky-larking again for a long, long time."

In the meantime, Toffee was staring back into the aisle, searching out the shelf on which she had last seen the infant Harpers. She made a little cry of surprise. The shelf was empty.

"They're gone!" she said. "They've gotten away. And after all the trouble we've gone through to bring those two crooks to justice!" A look of speculation crept into her eyes, and she turned to the nearest cop. She grabbed his arm with an urgent hand. "My babies!" she wailed dramatically. "My babies! They're gone. You've got to find them! You've got to! I'll kill myself!"

"What's that?" the cop asked mildly.

"I'll kill myself, Dumbo," Toffee said sourly. "Go get my babies. They've run away."

"I don't blame 'em. Where did they go?"

"How should I know?"

"Kill yourself, lady," the cop said tiredly. "I'm too worn out."

"Why you...!" Toffee started.

A sudden shriek from the foyer interrupted her. It was a scream with a purpose in life, it was ambitious, it was soul searing and nerve shattering.

In a body, the cops and the apprehended fugitives ran to the doorway. Then they stopped, completely stunned by the spectacle before them.

Two lank and very mature figures, clothed only to the essential degree in brief scraps of black velvet, were crawling serenely across the foyer floor. The ancient librarian, holding onto her counter to keep from slipping to the floor, was screaming her dreadful head off. The Harpers, apparently in the midst of escape, had suddenly and quite unbeknownst to themselves been restored to adulthood. At each movement the velvet wrappings were slipping a bit further afield. A number of people, some with books in their hands, were standing about the room in attitudes of fascinated bewilderment.

Beyond the apparent chronological transformation, even stranger changes had been wrought in the Harpers. Their faces were no longer the works of art that they had previously been. Agatha was definitely moon faced, in a wall-eyed, colorless sort of way, and Chadwick's handsome features appeared suddenly to have been run over by a steam roller.

"Holy gee!" one of the cops breathed, recovering from the first shock of surprise. "It's the homicidal Harpers!"

"What a catch!" his companion exclaimed excitedly. "We'll both get promoted, sure. Agnes and Chester Harper! They're wanted for things that ain't even got a name yet ... in five continents!"

In light of this sensational development, the ambitious policemen hastily abandoned their captives and started in pursuit of the Harpers.

Agatha and Chadwick, at the sound of running footsteps, glanced up, caught glimpses of each other and became instantly animated. Springing quickly to their feet, they frantically clutched their brief coverings to them where they would do the most good, and started to run, their bare feet slapping dully against the tiled floor. They raced through the entrance and out onto the sidewalk, the policemen in hot pursuit.

At the other end of the room Toffee plucked urgently at the sleeves of Marc and Mr. Culpepper.

"Why hang around?" she asked, motioning them back toward the bookshelves. "Follow me, men."

The three of them raced back to the aisle from which they had been so rudely ejected only a few moments before. They shoved the ladder to the far wall and hastily climbed toward the window. The window wasn't so accessible as it had been before the pillaging of the end bookcase, but they managed to reach it without too much difficulty.

Outside, the trio found themselves in a dead-end alley which was pleasantly bathed in bright moonlight. They did not tarry, however, to enjoy the scenery. Immediately upon hitting the pavement, Mr. Culpepper streaked out toward the sidewalk, and Marc and Toffee started out after him at a dead run.

Then something happened.

Ahead, they could see Mr. Culpepper skittering swiftly around the corner. Accordingly, it was only logical that they should be in the close vicinity of the little man's flashing heels. But they were not. Their own progress, unlike Mr. Culpepper's, suddenly lacked something in get-up-and-go.

Their steps definitely lagged, and their breath came to them in rasping gasps. As they ran, they turned questioningly to each other. Toffee screamed and stopped dead in her tracks. Marc came to a halt only a few steps distant. They gazed at each other in horror.

All at once, they had become nothing more than a couple of doddering old wrecks. Toffee, no longer a voluptuous young redhead, was now a withered, greyheaded hag. And Marc's transformation was no less startling, his clothes were hanging loosely over a shriveled frame that was noticeably hunched in the back. Both their faces were networked with wrinkles, and their eyes were dull with age. All of a sudden they had become old ... very old.

They stared at each other in silent bewilderment, too stunned to speak.

In this dramatic moment, footsteps thundered in the mouth of the alley, and the two policemen appeared, running toward them. The first to reach them, grabbed Toffee roughly by the arm.

"So!" he cried triumphantly. "Got yuh! Thought you'd pull a sneak, eh?"

"Hey!" the other cop yelled, arriving on the scene. "That ain't them!"

Toffee glanced quickly at Marc, then back at the cops. "Take your hands off me, young man," she cried indignantly. "Have you no respect for old age?"

"Gee, sorry, mother," the policeman said apologetically. "We thought you was someone else. Did you see a young couple with some babies runnin' down here?"

Marc shook his head. "Not a soul," he said.

The cops backed away, looking thoughtful.

"Say," one of them said, a note of suspicion in his voice. "What are you two doin' down here at this time of night?"

Toffee giggled coyly. "Why officer!" she exclaimed. "What a question!"

The cop looked shocked. "You're kiddin'," he murmured.

"It's our fiftieth anniversary," Toffee lied smoothly. "And right here, on this very spot, is where we first met. We thought it would be nice if we came back tonight." She reached out and patted Marc's hand with a pretty show of sentiment. "And it was, too, wasn't it, lover?" she asked.

"You two met in an alley?" the cop said, scandalized.

"Of course not," Marc put in quickly. "This was a park here in those days. Now, would you mind leaving us alone?"

"You'd better not stay here," the cop said. "These people we're looking for are still at large and they're clean outa their heads. You'd better go on home."

———————————

Marc and Toffee, accompanied by the cops, proceeded to the sidewalk, helping each other along in their sudden senility. They tottered up to the police car that was parked in front of the library and peered interestedly inside. Nearsightedly, they made out Agatha and Chadwick, sitting in the inner dimness, handcuffed to the door handles.

"What vile looking people!" Toffee exclaimed elegantly. "How vulgar. I abhor vulgarity, don't you, lover?"

"Indeed," Marc said primly. "Indeed I do, sweetheart."

Agatha's scowling countenance instantly appeared at the window. The woman opened her mouth to say something, then, at the sight of the aged couple, changed her mind. A suspicion of something too fantastic to believe flickered briefly in her eyes, then disappeared in a flood of doubt.

"Couldn't be," she murmured, sinking back into the dark reaches of the car. "But oh! how I wish it was!"

"What a disagreeable looking creature!" Toffee said. She turned pleasantly to the policemen who were standing proudly at her side. "See that they get everything that's coming to them, won't you, boys?"

"Yes, mam," the cops chorused. "We sure will."

Agatha's face reappeared in the window. "Say...!" she started hotly.

"Come, lover," Toffee said, turning to Marc. "Don't you think we should look for more refined company?"

As they started down the sidewalk, Toffee turned back and waved daintily to the two policemen.

"Goodnight, gentlemen!" she called.

"Gee," one of the cops said. "What a sweet old dame. It's sure a shame they got the wrong street."

"What do you mean?" the other cop asked.

"That alley they were in," the first cop said. "There wasn't no park there in the old days. There wasn't nothin' but a pickle factory. My old man used to work there." He sighed. "I didn't want to tell 'em ... might of spoiled their evening, you know."

For the enfeebled couple it was a long, tortuous climb to the fourth floor and to Marc's office. When they finally made it, they both collapsed into chairs and regarded each other bleakly.

"This is worse than being children," Toffee wheezed. "I could die."

"You may," Marc said morosely. "We've got one foot in the grave already. Anyway," he went on, "Agatha and Chadwick are taken care of."

"It hardly seems worth it," Toffee said, "when things turn out this way. No matter what punishment they get, it'll never be as bad as what's happened to us."

They both sat up as the door to the outer office whined open and slammed to. Footsteps rattled through the silence, and then the door to Marc's office edged open to make way for a small, ferret-like face.

"There he is," Toffee said. "The cause of it all. If I had the strength I'd strangle the little devil with my own two hands."

Mr. Culpepper looked at them with interest. "I was afraid this would happen," he said brightly. "I tried to warn you not to drink any more liquor, but you wouldn't listen. Now your chemical action has been reversed. If you'd only waited twenty-four hours you'd have been all right." He shoved the door open and stepped inside. "My!" he murmured, patting dust from his clothes. "I certainly had to run to get away from those cops. Why didn't you follow me?"

"We didn't have to," Toffee replied. "Thanks to you, there isn't a soul in the world who would recognize us."

"Yes, yes," Mr. Culpepper said, smiling. "We'll fix that up right away. I have it all worked out. If you take the original dose of two pills you should return to what you were before you grew old. And there shouldn't be any permanent after-effects."

"No!" Marc said. With a palsied hand he boosted his wasted frame out of the chair. "No more of those pills. Heaven only knows what they might do next."

"It could hardly be worse than what they've already done," Toffee said. "And besides, I won't stay this way for the rest of my life ... what little there is left of it. You'll take those pills if I have to fire them down your throat with a gun."

There were several heated exchanges before Marc finally gave in.

"Oh, all right," he said at last. "At this point I really don't care what happens anyway."

"The reaction will be faster this time," Mr. Culpepper said. "But don't be alarmed. Everything will be all right." He plucked two pills from the littered desk and handed them to Marc.

Marc frowned at the pellets for a long time. Then, saying, "Here goes everything," he popped them into his mouth. He turned to Toffee. "If we wind up in our infancy again, I'll...."

Suddenly he stopped; already Toffee's image was blurring before him. The blackness was closing in fast this time. The room seemed to whirl. Round and round it went, then it stopped with a jerk. But Marc didn't. He went sailing off into space ... into unbroken blackness....

Toffee gently removed her lips from Marc's and gazed at the quiet valley through half-closed lids. Folding her hands beneath her head, she lay back on the mossy grass. They were resting on the topmost point of the sloping knoll.

"You know," Toffee mused. "I'm actually a little glad to be back here this time. That business with the pills was rather fatiguing; we kept being such unattractive things. Oh, it was lovely being with you again, but here, in the valley of your subconscious, I can at least count on being what I am."

"I wonder," Marc said, "what age I'll be when I get back."

"Oh, you'll be back to normal, I'm sure," Toffee said. "When you stop to think about it, it should work out just as Mr. Culpepper said."

"Then I'll probably be dragged off by the cops the minute I show my face."

"Oh, I don't think so. No one really ever got a very good look at you. After the cops showed up, we were in the shadows most of the time and moving too fast. Besides they'll be looking for a couple with children."

Marc shrugged. "Maybe you're right." He sighed and stretched out on the grass at Toffee's side. "It's really very restful here," he said.

No sooner were the words out of his mouth than it happened, the earth began to rock beneath them. The little valley was seized by a spasm, it lurched crazily from side to side in an erratic see-saw motion. Marc dug his fingers into the grass, but it didn't help; in a moment he was rolling swiftly down the side of the knoll, heading into a thick bank of blue mist. Behind him he could hear Toffee calling to him, but her words were muffled and unintelligible though her tone was cheerful and unworried.

And then the mist closed over him, turned into fog and became dense and black.

―――――――――――

Someone was shaking Marc's shoulder when he opened his eyes, and he looked up into the anxious face of Mr. Culpepper.

"The girl!" Mr. Culpepper was crying. "Gone! Entirely gone. I didn't see her take any of the pills, but she's gone!"

Marc gazed dazedly around the room, heard himself echoing the word "gone."

"I didn't mean to do anything like this!" Mr. Culpepper wailed. "I didn't mean to destroy anyone."

To Marc, the room and his thoughts became clear in the same moment. He gazed at Mr. Culpepper's anguished face and smiled. Perhaps the little man deserved the remorse he was feeling; perhaps it was his just payment for tampering too much with the natural order of things. Still....

"I'm sure she's all right," Marc said. "She probably just wandered out when you weren't looking. She often does. Sometimes she just drifts away for whole months at a time. I wouldn't worry about it."

The little man looked up, smiled with relief. "She's so pretty," he said. "She's an awful heller but she's such a pretty one."

Two days later Marc was sitting at his desk, going through the morning mail, when Memphis opened the door and came in.

"The boys are here," she said.

"Boys?" Marc asked, looking up.

"You know. The applicants for the messenger boy job. There are several waiting. Shall I send them in?"

Marc dropped the letter in his hand and gazed absently out the window. "Oh, all right," he said. "Run them through."

Memphis left the room. A moment later there was a tap at the door.

"Come in!" Marc called without turning.

The door opened and footsteps moved into the room. There was a long moment of silence and then a throat anxiously cleared itself nearby. Marc turned around. A small boy, about twelve, regarded him from the other side of the desk ... a small boy with eager eyes and a hawk-featured face.

"Culpepper!" Marc yelled.

The boy twisted his cap nervously. "Yes," he said. "It's me, Mr. Pillsworth. Your secretary kept throwing me out."

"I told her to."

The boyish Culpepper nodded. "That's why I took the pills. It was the only way I could get in."

"There are several ways you can get out," Marc said menacingly. "One of them is with a broken neck."

Mr. Culpepper started waving his small hands. "You must listen to me, Mr. Pillsworth. I have something sensational to show you. You remember we were talking about something that would make people immortal? Well...." He paused to fish a small green bottle out of his pocket. "Well...."

"Out!" Marc was on his feet, yelling. "Out! OUT!"

The boy's eyes widened with alarm. He turned and scurried for the door like a frightened rat.

"Don't!" he shrieked. "Don't throw that paper weight, Mr. Pillsworth! I'm leaving, Mr. Pillsworth! I'm *leaving*!" He scooted through the door and slammed it after him.

Marc replaced the paper weight on the desk and sank back into his chair. For a long time he just sat there, staring blankly across the room. Then, slowly, a smile crept into his face.

Somewhere in the back of his mind there was laughter.

THE END

Milton Keynes UK
Ingram Content Group UK Ltd.
UKHW011145220424
441551UK00008B/838